Old Mother Hubbard

A Random House PICTUREBACK®

Alice & Martin Provensen

Old

Mother Hubbard

Random House New York

Library of Congress Cataloging in Publication Data: Martin, Sarah Catherine, 1768-1826. Old Mother Hubbard. (A Random House pictureback) *Summary:* Old Mother Hubbard runs errand after errand for her remarkable dog. 1. Nursery rhymes. [1. Nursery rhymes] I. Provensen, Alice. II. Provensen, Martin. III. Title. PZ8.3.M4150p 1977 398.8 76-24176 ISBN: 0-394-83476-3 (B.C.); 0-394-83460-7 (trade); 0-394-93460-1 (lib. bdg.)

Manufactured in the United States of America 10 9 8 7 6 5 4

OLD MOTHER HUBBARD went to the cupboard to fetch her poor dog a bone.

When she got there the cupboard was bare,

and so the poor dog had none.

She went to the baker to buy him some bread, but when she came back ...

the poor dog was dead.

She went to the joiner's to buy him a coffin, but when she came back . . .

the poor dog was laughing.

She went to the cobbler's to buy him some shoes, but when she came back ...

he was reading the news.

She went to the tailor's to buy him a coat, but when she came back...

he was riding a goat.

he went to the barber's to buy him a wig, but when she came back...

he was dancing a jig.

She took a clean dish to get him some tripe, but when she came back . . .

he was smoking a pipe.

She went to the seamstress to buy him some linen, but when she came back...

the dog was a-spinning.

She went to the grocer's to buy him some fruit, but when she came back . . .

he was playing the flute.

She went to the fishmonger's to buy him some fish, but when she came back ...

he was licking the dish.

Inside the image: STRAWS, BERETS, DERBIES, STOCKING CAPS, FUR, CAPS, BONNETS

She went to the hatter's to buy him a hat, but when she came back...

he was feeding the cat.

She went to the hosier's to buy him some hose, but when she came back . . .

he was wearing his clothes.

The dame made a curtsey.

The dog made a bow. The dame said, Your servant. The dog said,

BOW-WOW.